The Truth about those Billy Goats

First published in 2004 by
Franklin Watts
96 Leonard Street
London
EC2A 4XD

Franklin Watts Australia
45–51 Huntley Street
Alexandria
NSW 2015

A CIP catalogue record for this book is available from the British Library.

ISBN 0 7496 5728 6 (hbk)
ISBN 0 7496 5766 9 (pbk)

Series Editor: Jackie Hamley
Series Advisor: Dr Barrie Wade
Cover Design: Jason Anscomb
Design: Peter Scoulding

Printed in Hong Kong / China

The Truth about those Billy Goats

by Karina Law and Graham Philpot

Let me ask you something.

Do I look like a troll?

I may be short and fat, but I am no troll! Everyone knows that trolls live in caves or mountains. But I live by this bridge.

This was once a beautiful bridge. Sadly, with all the trip-trapping of hooves and feet, it has started to fall apart.

It's my job to look after the bridge and collect a small toll from passers-by. It's a very important job!

Porridge
OATS

The coins I collect go to the Woodland Council to help pay for repairs to the bridge.

WC

You may have heard some stories about me. Perhaps you know the one about the Billy Goats Gruff?

It isn't true!

There were three of them.
They were very gruff and very rough and very, very rude.

As you probably know, the Billy Goats Gruff were on their way to the next field. They liked the look of the grass there.

The smallest Billy Goat was the first to come trip-trapping over my bridge. He was a cheeky-looking kid with no respect.

I politely stopped him and asked him to pay the toll. "Get lost Troll!" he yelled, before barging straight past me. I was shocked!

Next, the medium-sized Billy Goat came trip-trapping over my bridge. He was a scruffy-looking goat with no manners.

I politely stopped him and asked him to pay the toll.
"Not on your nelly!" he rudely replied. I was disgusted!

Finally, the biggest Billy Goat came trip-trapping over my bridge.

He was a grumpy old goat with terrifying horns. I politely stopped him and asked him to pay the toll.

"TROLL!" he boomed gruffly.

"No, *toll!*" I repeated, thinking he had not heard me correctly.

"TOLL?" boomed the biggest Billy Goat, even more gruffly than before.

"Yes," I replied shyly. "Just a small charge to help pay for repairs to the bridge."

The biggest Billy Goat smiled.
It wasn't a very friendly smile.
"A charge you say?" he asked.
I nodded nervously.

Suddenly, the biggest Billy Goat charged straight at me and butted me over the side of the bridge!

SPLASH! I fell straight into the river. The biggest Billy Goat laughed gruffly.

He trip-trapped over my bridge to the other side of the river, leaving me soaking wet.

Thankfully, I never saw him nor any of the other Billy Goats Gruff ever again.

TOLL SHOP
How to COOK Goat STEW
GOAT STEW FOR SALE

Hopscotch has been specially designed to fit the requirements of the National Literacy Strategy. It offers real books by top authors and illustrators for children developing their reading skills.

There are 21 Hopscotch stories to choose from:

Marvin, the Blue Pig
Written by Karen Wallace
Illustrated by Lisa Williams

Plip and Plop
Written by Penny Dolan
Illustrated by Lisa Smith

The Queen's Dragon
Written by Anne Cassidy
Illustrated by Gwyneth Williamson

Flora McQuack
Written by Penny Dolan
Illustrated by Kay Widdowson

Willie the Whale
Written by Joy Oades
Illustrated by Barbara Vagnozzi

Naughty Nancy
Written by Anne Cassidy
Illustrated by Desideria Guicciardini

Run!
Written by Sue Ferraby
Illustrated by Fabiano Fiorin

The Playground Snake
Written by Brian Moses
Illustrated by David Mostyn

"Sausages!"
Written by Anne Adeney
Illustrated by Roger Fereday

The Truth about Hansel and Gretel
Written by Karina Law
Illustrated by Elke Counsell

Pippin's Big Jump
Written by Hilary Robinson
Illustrated by Sarah Warburton

Whose Birthday Is It?
Written by Sherryl Clark
Illustrated by Jan Smith

The Princess and the Frog
Written by Margaret Nash
Illustrated by Martin Remphry

Flynn Flies High
Written by Hilary Robinson
Illustrated by Tim Archbold

Clever Cat
Written by Karen Wallace
Illustrated by Anni Axworthy

Moo!
Written by Penny Dolan
Illustrated by Melanie Sharp

Izzie's Idea
Written by Jillian Powell
Illustrated by Leonie Shearing

Roly-poly Rice Ball
Written by Penny Dolan
Illustrated by Diana Mayo

I Can't Stand It!
Written by Anne Adeney
Illustrated by Mike Phillips

Cockerel's Big Egg
Written by Damian Harvey
Illustrated by François Hall

The Truth about those Billy Goats
Written by Karina Law
Illustrated by Graham Philpot